THE CLOWN
AND THE
CAREGIVER

THE CLOWN
AND THE
CAREGIVER

EDGAR J. HERN

Publisher's Cataloging-in-Publication Data

Names: Hern, Edgar J., author.
Title: The clown and the caregiver / by Edgar J. Hern.
Description: Las Vegas, NV: Amazon KDP, 2025.
Identifiers: LCCN: 2025905101 | ISBN: 979-8-9928840-6-7 (paperback) | 979-8-9928840-7-4 (ebook)

Subjects: LCSH Circus--Fiction. | Clowns--Fiction. | Horror
fiction. | BISAC FICTION / Horror /
General
Classification: LCC PS3608 .E76 C56 2025 | DDC 813.6--dc23

ESSENTIAL CIRCUS LINGO

beat back— The trapeze performer who swings back above the pedestal board

big top— The main tent used for performances

boss canvasman— The man whose job is to decide exactly where and how the tents should be put up at a new circus lot

bull handler— Circus employee working with the elephants

bullhook— A tool used by elephant handlers to manage and discipline them

carpet clown— A clown who works either among the audience or on the arena floor

cast out/force out— The far end of the first swing on a trapeze

catch bar— The trapeze that the catcher swings on

clown alley— Backstage area where clowns put on their makeup and store props

cutting up jackpots— Swapping tall tales about the circus

first of May— A novice performer in his first season on a circus show

flag— A vaulting exercise where the performer extends one arm and the opposite leg while facing forward with the chin higher than the shoulders.

fly bar— The bar the flyer (flying trapeze) uses

guys— Heavy ropes or cables that support poles or high wire rigging

harlequin— A diamond pattern with elongated shapes arranged vertically

hep/hup— Trapeze signal meaning "go"

king pole— The first pole of the tent to be raised that holds the peak of the tent

lista/listo— Trapeze signal meaning "ready"

lunge line— A long, single rein and the primary means of communication between the handler and the horse

lunge whip— A training device with a cord and pole that allows the equestrian to send the horse forward without needing to be on their back

main guy— Guy rope that holds up the center pole in the big top

remount— To return to the platform after swinging on the fly bar

ring horse— A horse that performs in the center ring and is trained to maintain timing despite distractions

surcingle— A strap or belt that fastens around the horse to secure the saddle or horse pack;

equipped with unique handles and a thick back pad for vaulting horses

towners— Townspeople, any outsiders

withers— Part of the spinal column that projects upwards between the shoulder blades of a horse

THE CLOWN AND THE CAREGIVER

Thursday, August 19, 2004. 8:46 a.m.

As the Texas sun beat down, a caravan of colorful circus trucks rumbled down Highway 83, their engines roaring in unison. The pulse of circus life reverberated through the North College district, miles from their destination. A storm of gravel coated everything in dust. Inside the trucks, the animals grew restless, their instincts bristling with anticipation. Lions paced with low growls that shivered through the air. Elephants trumpeted with excitement, their calls piercing the cacophony outside.

At the rear of the caravan, Susan, the bearded lady, navigated a long-bed pickup truck hitched to a 27-foot fifth-wheel RV. Her braids frayed into baby hairs, clinging like ground ivy to her damp skin. Hot breeze stirred her wild beard, itching her chin. Susan gripped the steering wheel, her focus unwavering as country music blared over the engine's rumble. The truck jolted over a pothole, its tires slamming against the wheel wells. She reached for a cup of iced soda, finding its chill a soothing break from the heat. Just as she raised it, another jolt sent soda splashing across her vintage harlequin blouse.

"Ugh, seriously?! Not again!" she exclaimed, glancing down at her blouse. With a frustrated sigh, she grabbed some napkins from the center console and dabbed futilely at the spill before it set.

On the bank of Elm Creek, a red-eared slider stood tall, its head raised. Its resolute stare fixed on the fast-approaching truck towing the fifth wheel. As the vehicle barreled down the highway, the turtle scurried away, yielding to the looming presence of the metallic beast that, like itself, carried a home on its back.

The clatter of the fifth-wheel hitch grating against the kingpin went undetected for miles under the cover of blasting music and roaring engines. A soft ping, barely audible, echoed with the drumbeat as the safety pin swung back and forth, rhythmically striking the locking bar with each jolt of the truck bed. The pin, which should have been locked in place, dangled precariously . . .

Dmitri, the strongman, and Lev, the little person, were inside the fifth wheel preparing breakfast. Lev set plates and flatware on the table while Dmitri, his muscles stretching the fabric of a white muscle shirt, called out, "How do you want your eggs?"

"Over easy, smothered in green chili sauce, please," said Lev, pulling a chair back.

Dmitri lifted the lid from a small bucket of lard and spooned some into the hot frying pan. It sizzled as he added a generous slab of bacon.

With a comical grimace, Lev asked, "Why must you use that stuff? Are you trying to turn me into a walking lard ball?"

Gingerly swirling the lard in the pan, Dmitri raised an eyebrow. He quickly turned, flexed his free arm, and said with a mischievous grin, "You see these muscles? I grew up eating lard all my life in Mother Russia, and this is how I turned out. If you eat lard, you can grow as big and strong as I am. Imagine the sheer power!"

"It's a little late for that," said Lev, gesturing to his short stature with a wave. "Now that you mention it, I sure miss Mother Russia."

"Да, я тоже," agreed Dmitri, adding eggs to the sizzling bacon.

Blissfully unaware of the calamity ahead, Susan roared past Lowden Street, singing along to her favorite tune. A slight left curve loomed ahead, its several waterlogged potholes waiting in quiet ambush. Taking another swig of her drink, she dropped the cup in the holder, tightened her grip on the steering wheel, and leaned into the turn. The kingpin heaved within the jaw coupling, unlocking the bar like a jail cell door.

The truck's front wheel plunged into a gaping pothole, unleashing a torrent of water and severing the kingpin from the jaw coupling. As the vehicle turned, the camper's loft slammed against the driver's rear quarter panel. Teetering precariously, the fifth wheel scraped against the asphalt before flipping. Susan's face was etched with agony as she watched the catastrophe through the rearview mirror.

"What the hell?" Dmitri's mind raced to comprehend the unfolding disaster.

"Aaagh!" Lev cried, paralyzed with fear.

The camper tilted ominously to the right. Dmitri desperately clutched the frying pan as the RV's sharp slope sent flames spilling into the hot lard. Grease burst into a wild inferno, flames lapping ferociously. Dmitri lost his balance and instinctively hurled the burning pan. It flew like a fireball, splattering grease across the sofa, which ignited in a burst of flames . . .

The screech of twisting metal and cracking fiberglass pierced Lev's eardrums, adding to the mounting chaos. He clung to the table as the world tilted and then flipped, his eyes widening with panic and mouth contorting in terror. The refrigerator doors swung open, sending the contents plummeting over him. Frozen in disbelief, he watched as leftover food in plastic containers, liter bottles of soda, and fruit bombarded him. The most dangerous were the beer bottles. They rained like giant hailstones, one striking his temple. The refrigerator plunged toward him, hitting the table with a loud thud, shearing it in two and pinning him against the wall.

"Help me!" he screamed as the cramped space darkened with smoke. He could feel the heat of fire behind him, roaring as it found more fuel, and filling his straining lungs with smoke . . .

Dmitri was thrown toward what had been the foot of the sofa, now the topside. Instinctively, his hands shot out to soften the impact, but one arm plunged into the searing flames. He recoiled, letting out a howl that tore through the mangled room. The fire raged, saturating the air with the stench of burning fiberglass. A metallic screech made him look up, just in time to see the range hurtling toward him. He leaped aside as it smashed into the door. Hearing Lev's pained cries, Dmitri sprang over the range, keeping his head low, dodging the smoke. His powerful arms wrapped around the refrigerator, lifting it clear off the table.

"Get out!" Dmitri yelled, veins in his temples popping.

Lev scurried out from underneath the unit, and the strongman dropped it back onto the table.

"There's no way out!" Lev shouted, his eyes wild as he coughed black smoke. "The camper landed on the exit side!"

Dmitri sprang onto the range, reaching up to open the sliding window. The opening wasn't large enough for his bulky body, so he ripped the tempered glass off their tracks. In the background, the fire popped and crackled menacingly as it advanced. Adrenaline surged, numbing him to the blackened burn on his arm.

"Get up here!" he called. Lev clambered up the range to where the strongman crouched, bracing himself. Dmitri grabbed Lev by the seat of his pants with his right hand. In one swift movement, he pushed off with his muscular legs and hurled his partner through the window like a shot put.

Arms flailing, Lev landed with a thump on the side panel of the fifth wheel, surprised by how hot the metal already was. He scrambled to his feet in time to see Dmitri push himself out through the window, swing his legs around, and jump off the vehicle.

"Time to fly like an eagle, little buddy!" Dmitri cried.

Lev took one step back and sucked a determined breath before hurling himself toward his friend. He soared through the air with his eyes shut and teeth clenched, landing in the waiting arms of the strongman, where he burst into tears. His heart beat against his smoke-filled lungs. *Damn, we almost died.*

Susan rushed toward them, her long braided hair swinging behind her, sobbing with relief. "Hurry! We have to get away from the camper!" she exclaimed, tugging at Dmitri's arm, Lev still crying over his shoulder.

As they ran toward the pickup truck, the propane tank exploded with a deafening boom, engulfing what was left of the fifth wheel in flames and flinging them all to the ground. Thick smoke, sepulchral black, billowed from the wreckage like a vengeful genie.

"Nothing is more alluring than the mystical forces of nature," said the strongman, gaping at the plumes rising from the twisted rubble.

Lev stared in a catatonic stupor, then started bawling again.

Dimitri was the first to recover his feet and set his partner upright. Lev looked up at him in awe. "I could've died back there. You saved my life, Dmitri," he said, his voice rising, as if to share it with the world.

"Don't mention it." For the first time, Dmitri looked down at the second-degree burns striping his arm. "You would've done the same."

"You mean I would've catapulted you through the air too?"

Dmitri tried to picture the image and shook his head. "I wouldn't recommend it. Not unless you want your little arm to go straight up my butt," he said with a satirical grin.

Lev grimaced.

Miles, the contortionist and driver ahead of Susan's rig, ran up, gasping for breath as he reached the pickup truck. His bald head gleamed in the light of the fire. "I radioed the lead driver," he said, his eyes flicking between them. "What the hell happened?"

Stroking her beard, Susan said, "I was making that turn there when the fifth wheel lurched and popped out from the hitch. It happened so fast!"

Miles walked to the truck's bed and inspected it. "Well, here's your problem," he said, puffing out his chest and pointing at the dangling safety pin. Lev scaled the twisted tailgate and hopped onto the bed as they all moved closer for a better look.

The strongman stared at the suspended safety pin with a befuddled expression. "That can't be," he said, raising a brow. "I rechecked the safety pin at the truck stop! Twenty minutes ago!"

"He's right," interjected Lev. "I saw him going through the protocol myself." He lifted his chin, daring anyone to discredit him. When no one did, he jumped off the bed and approached the contortionist. Scrutinizing Miles, he thrust his small finger out and said, "I wouldn't be surprised if this were sabotage!"

Everyone recoiled. Dmitri stepped back, tapping a thoughtful forefinger on his upper lip.

"And I have a damn good idea who it was," added Miles with a knowing nod.

Lev and Susan exchanged looks of knowing disbelief.

* * *

Kids teemed through Stevenson Park as parents shouted tips from the sidelines of a middle school baseball scrimmage. The coach cupped his hands around his mouth and yelled, "Play ball!"

The batter took his stance at home plate with fierce determination, muscles tensed, as the pitcher unleashed the ball. Then, with a resounding crack, the batter sent it sailing over the diamond. The ball arced high into the sky, losing momentum as it dropped toward the unprepared outfielder.

Mickey's glove was above his head, but with his attention fixed on the approaching vehicles down the road, the ball whizzed past him, landed in the scruffy grass, and rolled away. Cheers and boos from the crowd and frustrated shouts from his teammates erupted. Ignoring the noise, he dropped his glove and ran toward the mound. Mickey bounced on his toes and pointed at the road, crying, "A circus! The circus is coming! LOOK!"

Every head turned to see the fleet of semitrailers that stretched down East North 7th Street just outside the fence. A wave of kids swept to the sidewalk as they goggled at the kaleidoscopic panels advertising fearsome lions, towering elephants, and horses crowned with tossing plumes. The coach waved his arms and bellowed about teamwork in a futile attempt to regain control, but the allure of the circus was too strong. Even the parents were spellbound by the spectacle.

The trucks trundled into the vacant lot across from the park. Few locations in historic downtown Abilene offered a rare confluence of cultural amenities: the Spanish colonial Paramount Theatre, The Grace Museum, and most importantly, the public bathrooms at Stevenson Park.

"Stop right here," shouted Bill, his fist raised like an umpire calling strike three, his badass biker tattoo popping on his bicep. The truck's air brakes hissed as he zigzagged across the lot, directing the other drivers in their parking ballet. As the boss canvasman, he knew precisely where each tent needed to be in relation to the big top. Tightrope walkers huddled together, clowns clustered in a crowd, and acrobats stood in a ragged line, waiting for his word.

Bill brought his callused hand to his lips beneath a bristling mustache and whistled loudly. A snug white tank top accentuated his muscles, and his thick black beard, sprinkled with gray, was well-trimmed. "The king pole goes here," he said, raking the heel of his boot in an X in the dusty soil. "From this point, it will give us a radius of sixty feet, where the elephant trough rests. You know the floor plan, folks. Let's move!"

Knowing the routing, the performers scattered

to their tasks. Meanwhile, the delighted towners watched as four majestic elephants sauntered gracefully down the ramps, lending an air of grandeur to the bustling scene without the price of a ticket. The red-and-white canvas rose smoothly even without Susan, Dmitri, and Lev at their usual posts; they were busy with Highway Patrol and a recovery truck. Sturdy stakes were pounded into the hard ground to secure the guy wires that held the big top in place.

Bill hammered away, the clinking sound echoing across the grounds. Bubbles, the mischievous young calf from the herd, stood beside him, ready to assist. "This is a metal stake," he said, holding it up so the calf could touch it. "When I ask for a stake, you grab one and give it to me." His gentle grip guided Bubbles's slender trunk through the motions.

"Hi, Bill."

He paused the demonstration to look over his shoulder. "Hi Mila, how's your father?" he asked, giving the stake a few final whacks to secure it.

Taking advantage of the momentary distraction, Bubbles quenched his thirst from the nearby trough.

"I'm looking for Mr. Milagro."

"Well, he's not here right now." Bill shielded his eyes from the bright sun to look at the young equestrian. Her rich brown hair shimmered, making a halo around her face. "He's meeting with the Abilene City Council."

"I need someone to look at Mocha's off hind hoof. She's limping."

"No problem. I'll check it out as soon as I finish here," Bill reassured her.

"Thanks," she said, tilting her head with a smile. "I can help with the stakes if you like."

"That's all right. I already have a helper." He winked, a smile spreading across his tanned face. "Get this. I just trained Bubbles for this task. Watch." He whistled to the calf and held out his hand. "Bubbles, give me a stake."

Instead, Bubbles spouted a trunkful of water at him and scurried away. A wave of laughter rippled through the workers, Mila included.

By the time the sun nudged the western horizon, tents and rigging stood ready, awaiting the first show. Star performers and lowly clowns alike shared back slaps and congratulations. But the carpet clown, a short, bald man named Daniel Dewhurst, scowled at the merriment. His silence wasn't natural. It stemmed from the countless injustices that had plagued his life. His desolate eyes mirrored the look of listless vultures perched on branches of dead trees, waiting for the living to breathe their last.

Thirty-three workers struggled to keep the circus afloat, and Daniel was the unfortunate one assigned to dispose of all the animal waste, including elephant feces that towered over his wounded pride. He loathed the circus animals. Every last one of them. Especially Elsa, the largest of the four elephants, who had developed diarrhea in her old age, and Samson, the lion, who dumped the foulest steaming piles he had ever scooped.

Monday, August 23, 2004. 8:47 p.m.

One night, inside clown alley after a performance, Daniel removed his clown costume and dejectedly slipped into his old denim overalls. They were the softest, most comfortable overalls, but their frayed cuffs and rips in the knees were nightly reminders of his inadequacy and failures. Standing rigid in front of the mirror, he frowned at his receding hairline, a quiet monument to fading youth. His reflection filled him with shame and self-disgust. The mirror, a cruel accomplice, amplified his growing distaste for humanity. *Why? What did I ever do to be burdened with such a wretched existence?*

Over the years, his anger had twisted into envy toward the "normal," the young and con-ventionally attractive. *What a funny-looking man— and he never opens up to anyone,* they whispered, loud enough for him to hear. Their disdainful glances and unkind words only fueled his resentment. He yearned to teach them a lesson. To make them understand the pain he felt every time he peered into the mirror.

Daniel scooped up a sliver of soap from the grimy dish, working up the rich lather to strip off the clown makeup. It took several minutes to scrub away the unrealistically happy red grin. Streaks of crimson, black, and indigo intertwined in the washbasin, forming a swirl of despair—something straight out of an expressionist's nightmare. The haunting image whirlpooled into the drain with a screaming resonance.

"Look at you!" Daniel shouted, jabbing his plump finger at the reflection. His face contorted, teeth bared, grinding like a chisel against stone. "You're the Dung King of Texas!" He reached for a towel, and with a stare as vile as any rogue, he said, "What have you ever accomplished in your pathetic life?"

The mirror gave no answer, offered no comfort. "All you do is make half-witted children laugh and scoop up crap every night!" he snarled, his voice dripping with contempt and eyes blazing at his reflection's flaws. The damp cloth thudded against the mirror and crumpled into the sink as he stormed out.

Unbeknownst to Daniel, the trapeze artist, Hector Delgado, had been watching him through the tent's flap door. *This is one sick man*, he thought. *He's tormented. The poor guy doesn't realize every job is as vital as any other. Where would the world be without janitors?* Hector shook his head and turned to leave, only to freeze when he found Daniel standing before him, glaring.

"Were you spying on me, *Mr. Delgado*?" Daniel's voice was a low, threatening growl, his eyes boring into Hector's with malevolent intent.

"No," the trapeze artist replied, offering no details.

Daniel narrowed his eyes as Hector disappeared behind the tent.

* * *

Tuesday, August 24, 2004. 1:35 p.m.

The early afternoon crowd buzzed with anticipation. Mocha trotted rhythmically into the ring, her coat rippling like milk chocolate cascading down a fondue fountain, her mane and tail a whipped chocolate and cream garnish. A vaulting surcingle secured a thick pad snugly against her back.

Sheila, the lunger, expertly guided Mocha around the ring with the lunge line and whip. Showing no sign of a limp, the horse trotted rhythmically within the 15-meter circle, her white-bandaged legs rowing through the golden sea of hay.

Mila emerged from the shadows with poise, galloping into the light with the effortless grandeur of a Lipizzaner. The crowd was enchanted, swept up in the majestic strains of Johann Strauss's *Radetzky March*. She paused beside Sheila, the swish of her dark brown ponytail stilling. They took a moment to connect with the horse and ensure everything was set for the performance. Standing tall in her blue unitard, Mila took a deep breath and lifted her chin resolutely. *All those years of dance and gymnastics weren't for you to flop now.*

As Mocha completed her solo trot, the young

vaulter raised her arm, and the music changed to a lilting waltz. Timing her steps to the rhythm of Mocha's trot, she signaled, *Get ready. I'm going to mount.* Reaching for one of the surcingle's padded handles, Mila vaulted onto the horse's back with a swift motion, barely skimming an unusual bump in the thick pad. As the horse maintained a steady canter, she executed the mill with a series of leg swings, transitioning into other intricate poses that required immense core strength and control. Strips of fabric from her unitard whipped in the breeze as the 15-year-old extended her legs into a perfect split. With a gleam in her eyes, she swept down onto the pad, lifting her arms in triumph as the crowd erupted in cheers.

I got this!

Mila gripped the right surcingle handle and settled her left foot off-center along Mocha's spine, missing the raised spot in the pad. Facing forward, she stretched her right leg and left arm outward, executing the flag for four strides. More cheers cascaded through the big top as horse and rider soared around the ring like an arrow shot from an archer's bow. At the pinnacle of her performance, Mila sat back, her weight landing heavily on the horse for her final routine.

Mocha pinned her ears back with a snort, her eyes suddenly wide with panic. Her head dropped between her knees, and she bucked violently just as Mila's left foot swung down, catching in one of the leather loops. In an instant, the horse bolted forward, her mane a billowing banner as her powerful legs launched into a frantic gallop. In the chaos, the lunge line whipped through Sheila's fingers, searing red welts into her palms as she recoiled.

The sound of thundering hooves stunned the spectators into silence before gasps and murmurs rippled through the crowd. Sheila fought to stay calm, walking quickly across the ring to intercept the frightened horse.

"Ohhh!" the crowd screamed.

Numerous spectators cupped their hands over their mouths as they watched the helpless teenager being dragged by her snagged foot. Mila could feel the hay and dust kicked up by the horse's gallop, inches from her head. She thrashed her arms, trying to lift her shoulders and avoid the thrashing hooves.

Several performers ran into the ring and grabbed hold of Mocha's bridle, halting her movement. But it was Sheila's steady voice that calmed her, calling, "Easy, Mocha. Whoa, girl, easy now." She moved closer, offering gentle caresses and a carrot, easing the horse's agitation until her breathing slowed.

Meanwhile, Dmitri ran up and slid his strong arms under Mila's shoulders. Adrenaline quickened her breath. "My ankle!" she choked through gritted teeth. "I think it's broken."

Dmitri lifted her body slightly, allowing Lev to ease her foot out of the loop and gently place her leg on the ground. White-faced, she grimaced at the movement.

"You're okay, Mila. Lev is calling the paramedics now. You'll be riding on a merry-go-round in no time," he said jokingly.

Despite the pain, she managed a tight grin. "No way, Dmitri. I'm not going anywhere near a merry-go-round. They're much too dangerous."

* * *

Several minutes after the paramedics drove away with Mila, Sheila stormed into the room, roaring like a jungle king. She plopped the thick white back pad onto the folding table, where the other performers sat in Last Supper formation. Heads turned, eyes locked on her.

"Look at this, everyone!" she cried, her voice cut like a sour note. A stiff finger jabbed at the underside of the lining. "Someone wove a push pin under the pad. This wasn't an accident. It was an attack!"

Everyone gasped. Their horrified eyes fixed on the push pin protruding like an ice pick aimed at their morale.

Sheila's eyes burned with intensity. "For months, strange things have been happening, and no one seems to know who or what is causing them!"

As usual, Miles exuded calmness, sitting with his legs crossed behind his head. He gave a small shrug. "I have a pretty good idea who it was."

"Wait, are you suggesting it was the same person who caused the fifth wheel accident?" asked Susan. They locked eyes, the same thought passing between them. Then she pounded her fist on the table. "We need to report this to Mr. Milagro right away! Does anybody know where he is?"

"Joe went to the hospital with Mila to take care of the insurance paperwork," said Sheila, a muscle twitching in her jaw.

"Then it's time we took matters into our own hands!" Suddenly furious, Miles untangled his legs and stood up so fast his chair clattered over backward.

"Until we know for sure who is behind these accidents, we can't go lynching anyone," Dmitri warned, flexing his muscles to reinforce his authority. He raised his hand before his face, fingers splayed wide like a crocodile's gaping jaws. They snapped shut—once, twice—before opening again, mimicking the slow, deliberate bite of a predator. "We need to keep our eyes peeled, like a croc lurking in murky waters, ready to *snap!*" With a decisive clamp, his fingers snapped shut, sealing the point.

Heads nodded in agreement, except for Miles, who stepped defiantly toward Dmitri. "I'm telling you, it's the carpet clown!" he growled, his face red. "That guy has been suspect number one since his first of May! I'll wring his neck with my bare—"

"All right, all right. Don't get bent out of shape," Dmitri interjected with a glimmer in his eyes.

"What? Is that supposed to be some kind of joke?" Miles shot back, smirking.

* * *

Milagro Circus was not named after a miracle but rather for its financially troubled owner. Those who'd been around the longest jested that it was a miracle the circus had managed to keep operating. A tall and thin man, Joe Milagro appeared even taller with his black top hat perched atop his salt-and-pepper hair. Whenever he playfully wiggled his mouth, his long handlebar mustache went along for the ride, delighting children and occasionally exciting single women in the crowd. His pleasant eyes, as black as crude oil, crinkled with sincerity. For those fortunate enough to meet him, he often displayed a distinct mannerism—a cocked brow that signaled his genuine interest in their conversation.

To revive the failing circus, Joe had introduced a pig race: six pigs, six vibrant lanes, each color-coded to liven up the monotone seats and give every audience member a pig to root for. It was an expensive gamble, but one that quickly paid off.

It helped that each pig had a distinct personality. Chiquita was a tiny piglet, delicate as a seashell, adored although she never won any races. Cha-Cha was aptly named for her unique gait, which echoed the rhythmic flow of a Latin dance step. Marmalade earned her name after being found with her sizable snout stuck in a 5-ounce jar of orange marmalade, looking as embarrassed as someone walking into a glass door. Sassy, true to her name, was bold and lively. She was always the first to leap into the pool or challenge a bigger pig. Rosie's delicate pink skin rivaled rose petals, but her thorny demeanor made workers wary of her bite. Cleo earned her name from an Egyptian-style photo shoot, where she was fitted in a gold-trimmed skirt and poised on a red velvet Cleopatra sofa, legs crossed regally. Joe built a playpen for his six superstars on an old flatbed trailer, featuring a small vinyl pool with a wooden ramp and even a small slide.

Spectators lingered after each show to admire the animals, especially the fierce predators. This didn't sit well with Abilene city officials, already wary of granting a four-week permit near Stevenson Park. Had Joe not assured them everything would run smoothly, the circus might've ended up pitching tents in dusty Moreno Valley, west of Palm Springs and north of San Diego.

* * *

Thursday, August 26, 2004. 9:48 p.m.

No fearsome growling tonight. No ripping of flesh into chunks. The tigers were out cold, the horses snoozing comfortably. Crickets chirped in the distance as the man in the moon cast his watchful gaze over the sleeping Earth.

Daniel climbed the ladder to the pigpen and opened the gate, startling the gentle creatures from their slumber. If anything could trigger misophonia, the shrill cries of pigs were undoubtedly among the worst. His blood boiled as he gripped the shovel, raising it over his head.

"Shut up, you damn motherless swine!" he shouted, his eyes bulging with rage. Spittle spewed from his mouth, riding the air like venom on the wind.

Daniel lunged forward and immediately slipped on a pile of feces. His leg zigzagged like a novice ice skater, but he regained his footing, swearing. "I'll get the best of you, you damn critters!" he fumed, scraping his shoe against the truck bed. The shovel swung from side to side, each swing more violent than the last. Tension gripped his frame as the shovel clashed against the flatbed, sending sparks flying.

Squealing, Chiquita dashed up the ramp and jumped into the pool, as if *that* was any escape. Sassy was right behind her, followed by Marmalade, whose bulk splattered Daniel's legs. Cha-Cha grunted a warning and lunged at the intruder's leg, sending him stumbling back in surprise. Before she could scurry away, he struck her hind leg with a sharp crack of the shovel. Cha-Cha's squeal pierced his eardrums, snapping him back to his senses. The other pigs joined in a bizarre cacophony as Cha-Cha hobbled out of reach.

Joe was tabulating the day's receipts on his clunky keyboard calculator when cries filtered through the trailer's window screen. He shoved his top hat on at an angle and threw on his red coat. Stepping outside, he found the boss canvasman already in motion.

"What's going on?" Joe bellowed.

"I don't know. Something's upset the pigs," Bill said, his chest bare and a towel slung over his shoulder. He quickened his pace to keep up with the ringleader's whooping crane steps. Ahead of him, the lapels on Joe's coat flapped with every stride, then fell flat as he stopped short. Just beyond them, Daniel was already halfway up the truck's ladder, clutching Cha-Cha in his arms.

"Dan!" thundered Joe over the pigs' squeals. "What in tarnation is going on here?"

"Mr. Milagro," Daniel said, looking guilty.

Cha-Cha lifted her snout, curled her nose, and her eyes gleamed with joy at the sight of her valiant savior. She struggled to free herself from the clutches of the clown.

"I went in to clean the pigpen, but Cha-Cha ran out when I opened the gate. It wasn't my fault. She jumped off the truck and hurt herself when she hit the ground." Daniel's beady eyes darted between the two men, watching to see if they'd buy his story.

Joe nodded, disbelief plain on his face. "Bill, take the pig and have a look at her leg," he said, squinting at Daniel.

Bill cradled the pig gently in the crook of his elbow. Cha-Cha snorted softly, nuzzling his bicep for comfort. His fingers probed the injured leg, checking for bruising. She flinched when he touched a spot already turning black and blue. He traced the length of her leg, feeling for her pulse, assessing whether the break had damaged any blood vessels.

"It's the fibula, all right. It's broken," he said, shaking his head and shooting the ringleader an I-told-you-so stare. "Cha-Cha won't be racing anytime soon."

"It's not my fault, Mr. Milagro," Daniel insisted, jumping off the ladder and kicking up a cloud of dust around his shabby deck loafers. "I swear on my father's grave, it's not my fault!"

Joe turned to Bill. "Get someone to help with a splint and take Cha-Cha to the nearest vet."

Glad his partner had finally seen the obvious, Bill departed with the injured pig nestled close. Cha-Cha snuffled softly as if to thank the ringleader for his most judicial decision.

Daniel opened his mouth to protest his innocence, but the boss had had enough.

"Stop right there!" Joe's voice boomed, making Daniel flinch. "I will not tolerate any more accidents!" He pointed his double-jointed finger. "I don't know what you're up to, Dan, but every time something goes wrong, you're always right there with some lame excuse!"

The corners of Daniel's lips curled downward. "I had nothing to do with Cha-Cha's broken leg," he repeated, hiding behind indignation.

"Nevertheless," Joe scrutinized him. "This is your last chance. I'm holding you fully responsible for every animal's well-being. If anything else happens, and I mean *anything*, you are through!"

Daniel stood rigid while Joe tilted his head back. For a moment, the threat of physical violence hung thick between them. The carpet clown considered the drawback of a traveling circus. *I'm too far from home to lose my job over a pig. And who knows where we might end up? I'm sure as hell not trekking back to Hastings by myself!* Dropping his gaze, he was quick to acquiesce.

The ringmaster cocked a brow and watched Daniel slink off, like a sly coyote with a jackrabbit in its mouth, keeping a wary eye out for larger predators that might steal his kill. The clown shot a sideways glance back before vanishing behind a trailer. Joe exhaled hard and surveyed the skies, his black top hat leaning at an astonishing angle without falling off his brilliantine-slicked hair. He closed his eyes, recalling the night the canvasman had warned him about the clown.

Monday, June 17, 2002. 10:07 a.m.

"Explain why you think I shouldn't hire him," Joe had replied, throwing his soon-to-be-donated pickup truck into fourth gear. The rusted red truck rattled and squeaked over the rough terrain of southern Nebraska, shuddering like a small plane in a downpour.

Bill clutched the grab handle above his head. "There's just something about his eyes that doesn't sit right," he said, staring out the window, his body swaying with the truck. "He's evil, I tell ya. I've got this bad feeling about your plan to launch the circus, with him around."

Reluctant to assume the worst, Joe brushed his well-defined chin and turned his head, spitting out the window. "I feel it's only fair to give the guy a chance. I think I'll *recruit* him," he said, wiping the tobacco drip away. "Everyone deserves a chance. If I were in his shoes, I'd want an opportunity too."

"But you're not in his shoes," Bill retorted, crossing one leg over the other.

The truck hit a pothole, and Joe yanked the steering wheel, straightening the vehicle. "Let's give the guy a few months to prove himself."

* * *

Hector Delgado hungered for the adventure and excitement only a circus could provide, and the thrill of the catch ultimately drew him to the trapeze. One could glimpse unfathomable passion in the dark pools of his eyes. His father was the first to recognize this irrepressible yearning and encouraged his son to travel alone to Australia for trapeze training at seventeen. Hector pursued a once-in-a-lifetime opportunity after signing a release form. The talk around the community was that his father had planned to rid himself of his son after his wife's sudden death. But making that decision was the most meaningful thing he'd ever done for his son. Fortunately, only those dear to him grasped the good that sprang from his heart.

Upon returning to the States in 1971, Hector, ripped from vigorous training, pursued his passion with a local circus. There, he met Veronica Small, whose yardstick-straight posture and unnaturally clean hair—like it might squeak when rubbed—struck him as both elegant and surreal. He fell hard.

Their relationship quickly led to marriage and three daughters. Jessica, the first to bring him joy, had her mother's gentle eyes. Jill, built for distance like a giant Asian flying squirrel, dreamed of soaring like an eagle over orange and purple canyons on a languid winter's eve. Then came Cecily. She was born too soon, her lungs fragile, her survival uncertain. Hector spent five months at her side and vowed never to let harm near her again.

Saturday, August 28, 2004. 10:02 p.m.

After admiring the Texas sky, Hector and Cecily had fallen asleep on their folding chairs. A low growl—too close for comfort—jolted him awake. Blinking away the haze, Hector spotted Samson barely twenty-five feet away, the tufted tip of the lion's tail twitching as it sniffed the air. Without looking away, he gently nudged his daughter and clapped his hand over her mouth. Slowly, he raised a finger to his lips, then pointed at the escaped predator. When she saw the massive lion, Cecily's face stiffened with fear.

Then the beast roared, striking a chord in Hector's spine. *We've been spotted.* Both father and daughter immediately froze, barely breathing. Samson's large amber eyes were alert, and his tail jutted out with the tip curved upward. He growled and took a calculated step forward.

"Cecily," Hector said softly. "See that truck over there?"

She nodded, her body trembling with a raw fear.

"We're going to walk slowly toward it. When we get halfway, I want you to run to the truck, get inside, and close the window. Do you understand me?"

Cecily glanced at the truck. It seemed impossibly far away. She wasn't sure her legs would carry her that far. "I can't, Dad," she said, her voice quivering.

"Yes, you can, sweetheart." Hector rose and grabbed his chair, holding it like Rocco during a live performance, pointing its four legs forward to confuse the single-minded lion. *Crack! Pop!*

Voicing the sounds with each snap, he lashed out with an imaginary whip. Samson growled, stepped back, then assumed a fierce stance. His eyes were glued on Hector and Cecily as they crept toward the truck. *Crack!* Hector cast the imaginary leather rope, and the lion responded by slashing the air with razor-sharp claws. The more Samson pressed, the harder Hector whipped the air.

"Now, Cecily!" he cried.

"Aaaagh!" She bolted.

Samson roared and charged, flinging dirt into the air.

Hector threw the chair to the ground and lunged forward, driving his legs and hips into a tackle against the lion's ribcage. Catching him in mid-leap, Samson hit the ground with a loud thump and rolled under the truck. With the wind knocked out of him, the lion struggled for breath, his chest rising in shallow bursts, his head lifting groggily.

Hector bolted to the front of the truck, shouting at his daughter to close the window.

"Dad!" she wailed, panic blooming behind her eyes.

"Roll up the window!" he ordered again.

Cecily crouched over and cranked hard. Suddenly, Samson's claw slashed through the opening, snaring a lock of her hair. A mighty roar boomed inside the cabin like thunder, and Cecily shrieked, her trembling hand fighting the crank. With her free hand, she repeatedly pounded out two short and one long blasts on the horn, the final note stretching longer each time.

Hector scrambled onto the truck's container. "Samson!" he bellowed, clapping his hands. For a moment, the predator's gaze locked onto him. They stared each other down, challenging the other to back down and show who had the biggest balls.

Hector gritted his teeth and shouted, "Come on, you son of a bitch. I know you want me as much as I want you." He roared without breaking eye contact, "Come on!"

Samson's mane shimmered in the moonlight as

he shook his head. He roared fiercely and withdrew his large paw from the window, allowing it to close completely. He sprang onto the hood, contorting it, and it snapped back into shape when he leaped onto the container. Hector slowly backed away. The lion's growl was deep and slow—he knew the hunt was over. His strides were measured and deliberate, his menacing presence undeniable.

Hector had nowhere to go. Even if he jumped off the container, Samson would surely follow—his jaws aiming for his neck. He held out his left hand and cracked the imaginary whip with the other. The lion roared and slashed at the air, crouching on his powerful hind legs . . .

Samson lunged at his prey.

Hector thought he had heard a rifle discharge when he fell back, but he had no time to process it. The lion's full weight sprawled over him, pinning him against the container. As he shoved the massive body off, his eyes landed on the tranquilizer dart embedded in Samson's neck.

Shaken and bruised, he staggered to the edge of the container.

Hector rubbed the back of his neck, trying to shake off the adrenaline. He huffed and said, "Do you always show up late for parties?"

"Depends who it's for," Joe replied, standing in front of several crew members who had convened behind him, their faces tense and dust-streaked.

Cecily clambered out of the truck and ran to her mother while Hector climbed down.

The ringleader snatched his top hat off the ground, shaking the dust from its brim. "Rocco, how did that lion get loose?" he asked, settling it firmly onto his head.

"No clue," responded Rocco, his eyes narrowing with suspicion. "I check the cages after each performance, without fail."

"Where do you keep the key?"

"It's on a hook by the door in my trailer," Rocco said, his voice clipped and impatient. "I told Emilio I'd dice up the onions for tomorrow's stew. I only stepped away for an hour."

A ripple of unease passed through the crew as they edged closer. Bill couldn't contain himself. "Someone could have grabbed the key and placed it back without your knowledge," he said.

"But why?" Rocco hesitated, his brow furrowing. "Why would anyone do such a thing?"

Joe swept his gaze across the crowd, calculating who was present . . . and who wasn't. He turned briskly to Rocco and said, "Take a couple of men and get Samson back in his cage."

"Yes, sir," Rocco replied, quickly gathering help.

"Are you thinking what I'm thinking?" Bill asked.

"Say no more."

Joe and Bill hurried toward Daniel's trailer, their footsteps crunching on the dry grass underfoot. Under the dim circus lights, the small, egg-shaped trailer sat with its peeling paint and crooked steps, looking comical in the gloom.

Fueled by rage, the ringleader flung the door open without knocking. Inside, they found the carpet clown sprawled on his cot, a whiskey bottle slack in his grip. He had drunk himself into a stupor, the trailer thick with the stench of alcohol and other offensive odors.

"Daniel, wake up!" Joe barked.

Bill kicked at him with his steel-toed boot, but after several blows, Daniel didn't stir. The bottle hit the floor, spilling the last of its whiskey.

"Never mind, Bill," said Joe, tugging at his shoulder to stop further abuse. "He's wasted. Must've been in this state since finishing his rounds. It must not have been him." *We can stay up all night cutting up jackpots, but this will be the icing on the cake!* They left Daniel's trailer in disgust, flicking off the light before slamming the door.

As they hurried off, Daniel overheard Bill arguing that the clown was the one who set the lion free: "That lousy piece of shit does nothing but gripe all day. I'd bet my life it was him. Even if he's drunk out of his skull!"

Daniel lifted the blinds to peek through, a sly grin creeping across his face. Relishing his drunken act, he thought, *Good, I kept those two characters off my back.*

* * *

Sunday, August 29, 2004. 4:05 p.m.

Joe felt the pinch. Without the pig race, he'd been forced to cut wages by 30 percent across the board and halved his own pay. The circus crew accepted the drastic decision instead of dropping two employees.

"We must reduce our expenses by any means possible," Joe said, his hands fiddling nervously with the fringed sash. His eyes were bloodshot, with dark circles hinting at sleepless nights. "I'm open to ideas," he said, his voice laden with defeat.

"How about we reduce the animals' food rations?" Rocco asked jokingly.

"I'll personally feed you to Samson before we do that," said Bill, turning to Joe. "These animals are my family, and we're responsible for their welfare."

"W-why don't we bring back the p-p-pig race and put Gypsy in place of Cha-Cha? Is-is there a Texas law that says goats can't im-im-impersonate pigs?" asked Marty Lewis, better known as Jo-Jo the clown. "She can fill the missing color slot!"

Laughter rippled through the group. At first, it was a silly notion, but as Joe considered it, the idea began to sound plausible. Marty beamed, soaking up the accolades and thumbs up he'd kicked into high gear. His thin face nodded repeatedly, his protruding chin exaggerating his grin. To keep the momentum going, he added, "W-we can . . . We can put a rubber pig nose over Gypsy's. You know . . . " Marty swallowed hard and took a deep breath. "J-j-just like the ones they sell at gag stores, the ones with the elastic bands. We could even get rubber pig ears!"

The more he spoke, the more energized they became, realizing they had a chance to turn the circus around. Marty's heart was beating fast. *Wow, I'm the first to present a great idea, not the usual loudmouth lion tamer!*

News of the reinstated pig race hit local radio stations the next morning, along with a front-page headline on the Abilene Foremost. See the mysterious sixth pig! read the flyers, posters, and banners. Much to the ringleader's delight, attendance at the day's performances skyrocketed.

Friday, September 3, 2004. 11:27 a.m.

There were no clouds in the sky to form cotton ball figures. Gone were the Chihuahuas, bears, and furry bunnies that drifted across the blue sky. Vanished were the dolphins, whales, and jellyfish that floated in the sea. The wind had erased them forever, as if a giant toy had been shaken, wiping the sky clean of every sketch and swirl.

Wearing denim overalls, Daniel stood before the washbasin and splashed cool water on his face and back. As it trickled down his skin, a smile crept across his face, a rare sight. Seeing a black swan in the Sahara might've been more likely. Grabbing a comb from his rear pocket, he brushed his thinning, wet hair to one side with a trembling hand, then dried his face. The mirror reflected a lonely man filled with insurmountable hate, a hallucinating mind, fashioning ideas only *he* could comprehend. A cold breeze swept through the room, causing the hair on the back of his neck to stand on end.

Two ghostly tentacles, their ethereal forms writhing, reached out from the mirror's depths, hovering over him like serpents poised to strike. Paralyzed, Daniel watched as they moved, wrapping around him with predatory swiftness. One slithered across his face and clamped over his mouth, stifling his scream, while the other coiled behind him, dragging him forward. The mirror rippled like a secluded forest pond, disturbed by droplets from a branch. A dark, swirling cloud seeped from its depths, twisting into an amorphous shape with eerie fluidity. Its presence spread like a creeping shadow, casting unearthly menace into every corner.

No longer struggling against the mysterious force, Daniel allowed the tentacles to sway his body, hypnotizing him. He stared into the mirror, mesmerized by the demonic entity that swirled in a whirling, ever-changing pattern. *A murmuration of starlings*, he thought. Tendrils of black fog wove together, their edges dissolving into the air only to reassemble into sinister new forms. Two black pits flickered into existence as eyes, burning with ancient wrath. A gaping maw yawned open, as if to swallow him whole. The creature released a low, guttural growl, its breath whipping Daniel's hair back like a tempest's warning.

A strange calm washed over Daniel as the creature loomed closer. Silence hung between them. The evil in its eyes burrowed into his frail mind like a dark seed taking root, spreading through his thoughts and weaving itself into his being. Drawn to the seductive pull of malevolence, he chose the easy path. *If it's chaos you want, then chaos you shall have . . . as long as I'm spared.*

Soon the tentacles released him, dissipating

into the stale air. Daniel stood, aware of what had transpired. A strange connection lingered, as though their thoughts had begun to intertwine. And the message was loud and clear. Walking away in a trance, he felt the entity fade, his sinister grin lingering like an echo of what had taken root.

Daniel reached for the pail and shovel he despised, clanking them to alert the animals he was coming. With a sneer, the clown went to work as if nothing had happened.

Play, a healthy behavior, is a common language between the wind and pennant. The prevailing winds willingly engage with the eight triangular pennants high above the big top, teasing them, one by one, and gently nudging them for attention. In response to their reluctance, an intense gust quickly awakens them from their slumber. Soon, a playful dance ensues, like two pups meeting for the first time. The pennants flap their tails in unison, flirtatiously daring the wind to keep up. They master the art of whipping their tails without harming the wind and learn to communicate with other pennants. Their steady rolling and waiving, now in

full swing, enhance the coordination that will carry them through the day.

* * *

11:55 a.m.

Elsa had been with Milagro Circus since its inception, dazzling audiences with her performances. She had mastered the fundamentals of raising the big top. At each new location, she eagerly handed metal stakes to the workers and used her immense power to hoist the towering supports that kept the tent fabric taut. It was a feat that had earned the elephant star status among the circus workers. But that was months ago.

Her ambition waned after she withdrew from the herd. Elsa had fallen ill, plagued by foul-smelling diarrhea. Knowing she was near death, Joe Milagro placed her, unrestrained, in a small private tent to ensure her comfort during her final days.

Throughout that sweltering day, she stood languidly in the middle of a brown, water moat while a swarm of flies teased her relentlessly. Tears trickled down Elsa's withered face, her long eyelashes clumping like wet pasta. There were no stars in her eyes, only sorrow and grief. With no remedy for the arthritic elephant, it was only a question of time.

When Daniel opened the tent flap, the blood drained from his face, and his heart lurched at the overpowering stench. In an apoplectic fit, he threw down the pail and shovel with a thud and a clang.

"Holy shit!" he exclaimed, sprinting up and down Elsa's length. He cursed and blasphemed. His eyes bulged beneath furrowed brows, and his nostrils flared with fury. Grabbing the weather-beaten shovel, he yelled, "There's no way in hell I'm going to clean up this filth!"

One hundred billion outraged neurons ran amok. He swung the shovel like a baseball bat, striking the elephant's withered rump, the blade tearing through her thick skin. Elsa's eyes became crazed. She trumpeted fiercely and struck Daniel on the shoulder, sending him soaring across the tent. The pail spiraled away as his body struck it.

Daniel climbed shakily to his feet and brandished the shovel like a sword. "Stay away from me, you beast!" he shouted, ignoring the cut on his arm. The sounds of laughter and applause from the big top faded into a distant murmur, overshadowed by the low, rumbling growl of an enraged Elsa. Breathless and rattled, he thought only of saving the audience from the turmoil he had unwittingly unleashed. In one frantic motion, he flung the handle aside and bolted toward the exit.

Instead of steering the rampaging elephant away from the public, Daniel ran through the rear entrance of the big top with Elsa in close pursuit.

"Get out!" he shouted. "Everyone out! Elsa's gone mad!"

Under the big top, the Delgado family was halfway through their trapeze routine. Cecily arced gracefully through the air on her return, executed a 180-degree turnabout, and caught the approaching bar with unwavering precision. After completing the shooting star, she landed smoothly on the pedestal board beside her sisters. On the edge of their seats with bated breath, the audience cheered and applauded . . .

The deafening roar of the crowd drowned out Daniel's frantic cries. With their attention focused overhead, no one noticed him stumbling into the center ring, let alone heard a word.

Elsa rammed the red aluminum bleachers like a freight train, sending people flying; popcorn and soda cups showered the crowd.

"It's raining!" a small child cried. The boy's father looked up, startled, and tried to shield his son from falling bodies. Pandemonium spread across the tiered seating like fire. Frightened spectators scrambled to escape from the twisted wreckage . . .

"Lista!" shouted Hector.

Gripping the fly bar, Cecily launched off from the pedestal board, gaining momentum as she swung downward toward her father. As always, the cast out electrified her with the freeing sensation of flight, lighting her with joy. A tingle spread through her feet as she extended her toes to tickle the underside of the canvas. Her father swung up and above the pedestal board during her back beat, then she plunged for her trick . . .

Dazed and disoriented, Elsa wrapped her trunk around a man who sprawled at her feet and thrust him back into the audience. He landed awkwardly but safely on top of two women several rows up, bumping his peach-fuzz scalp. Spectators shrieked at the unscheduled show as the elephant trumpeted and hammered her ribbed trunk against the metal rail, inciting a general panic. Elsa continued thumping, demanding attention and respect. The crowd pushed and shoved one another, some trampling others like battered doormats.

Sweat glistening on his brow, a bull handler stepped forward with a bullhook to push Elsa back. He jabbed repeatedly at her face but she fought fiercely. She smacked him across the face with her trunk, knocking the bullhook and his baseball cap aside. *I've never seen Elsa behave like this!* Another strike on the shoulder sent him reeling to his knees. He held his arm over his head to blunt the next blow when Daniel appeared with another bullhook. Dodging Elsa's waving trunk, the carpet clown forced the elephant back with the tool, allowing the battered bull handler to get up. Working together, they pushed Elsa toward the center ring, clearing a path to the rear exit for the panicked people . . .

"Hup!" Oblivious to the mayhem below, Hector signaled for his daughter's release. Cecily's baby-blue leotard glittered as she flew through the spotlight. Hanging upside down from the catch bar, he reached out and clamped his hands on her wrists. During their back beat, her eyes glistened with delight. But as they swung forward, he saw a look of concern cross her face.

Something's wrong, she realized, as screams and angry trumpeting sounded below. When Hector released his daughter for the return, she broke the first rule of flying: Instead of locking her eyes on the approaching bar, she glanced down . . .

Daniel and the bull handler kept prodding Elsa away from the crowd. Confused by their shouting, she lost her footing and stumbled backward into the massive king pole, her colossal weight splintering it like a rotten twig . . .

Cecily's arms flailed, but it was too late. The trapeze bar swung toward her, but she wasn't in position to catch it. Three fingers grasped at the bar, straining to get a grip even as she knew it was futile. In slow motion, she watched the ring finger slip off, followed by the pointer, leaving a single finger holding her weight. The world seemed to rotate in slow motion. Her father's frantic shouts, the audience's screams, and the trumpeting below faded to silence. Only the thudding of her heartbeat remained. Gravity and the angle of the swing defeated her grip. She dropped feet first.

Cecily's toes hit the platform, her heels hanging in midair. Suspended for just a moment, she shrieked, arms flailing, as Jill, Jessica, and Veronica reached out and pulled her to safety.

Her mother gazed into her frightened eyes. "And where do you think you're going?" she asked, pulling her into a tight embrace . . .

Too weak to stand, Elsa pushed with her hind legs but fell back, further damaging the king pole. The strain snapped two main guy wires, their sudden failure sending the pole shifting violently, cracking like a giant nutcracker's grip. It growled as it leaned to a precarious 30-degree angle, working loose several metal stakes and forcing the tent to droop inward. Eight guy wires shuddered under the immense strain, barely keeping the pole from collapsing onto the crowd. The floodgates to pandemonium had been opened, and spectators scattered in every direction.

The bull handler barely had time to brace before Elsa's trunk slammed into him, flipping him onto his back in a cloud of dust. His heart beat frantically as he rolled onto all fours and peered at the bullhook just out of reach. A drop of blood fell from his split lip and darkened the ground between his hands. *This is not the Elsa I know.*

Amid the chaos, three figures burst into the center ring. Lev and Susan shouted to distract Elsa while Dmitri snatched up the bullhook. With Daniel staggering beside him, Dmitri helped drive the elephant back from the fallen handler. But Elsa spun, her eyes locking onto Susan; then she charged.

Screams echoed as Susan stumbled and slammed to the ground, hay tangling in her frizzed-out hair and mouth. Dmitri grappled with Elsa, moving to protect his fallen comrade. Despite his size, Lev rushed forward to help Susan, who could not stop coughing. Just then, Elsa struck Dmitri a fierce blow to the head, sending him reeling as his vision faded into a sea of stars.

Locking eyes with her aggressor, the elephant rushed Daniel. She blared her trumpet with a discordant, sour tone, striking the bullhook from his grasp and sending it soaring several feet. Her distressed black eyes took in the chaos. An unspeakable fear rippled through the big top—

one she'd never seen before. Elsa swung her head from side to side, uncertain. She had not meant for this to happen. She played her trumpet to say *Don't be alarmed! I'm not going to hurt you!* Then her eyes found Daniel again, and grievance swelled. She resumed her trumpet playing, reaching higher notes that meant: *This is the man who started it all! He brought on my pain and suffering. He is the one to blame!* She couldn't have said it plainer, but no one was listening. No one cared about her cries of injustice, nor did they try to understand her pain or offer sympathy.

Scrambling to retreat, Daniel tripped and fell, knocking the wind out of his lungs. Elsa lumbered to him, her trumpet sounding with unprecedented intensity. Her left foreleg lifted, ready to smash Daniel's head into the ground.

Blood splattered Daniel like warm summer rain and streaked him with red paint after a mighty thunderclap. His pupils dilated as Elsa towered over him. While her raised foreleg hovered, her trunk unexpectedly went limp. Blood streamed down her rough, wrinkled face as she slowly tipped over like a giant sequoia. Purely on instinct, Daniel rolled to escape the elephant's bulk. The ground shook from the impact of Elsa's 8,000 pounds, sending up a cloud of hay and grit. When the dust settled, they were eye-to-eye, inches apart.

Daniel closed his eyes in relief.

Elsa closed her eyes in death.

The magnificent creature was dead, and Joe ached to know he would never hear her trumpet again. Smoke from the elephant rifle lingered in the air, permeating his clothes and skin. Though her death saddened him, he was relieved Elsa would no longer suffer the ravages of old age. *If only I could be so lucky.* In silent tribute, the circus owner removed his top hat and treasured red coat, laying them beside her massive, lifeless body.

A single tear streaked through the dust on Joe's face.

✳ ✳ ✳

High above the circus top, where the severed king pole came to rest, the single black pennant hanging from its tip no longer danced in tandem with the playful wind. It lay limp and lifeless—for no fun is to be had when death takes center stage.

* * *

The next day, the headline from the Abilene Foremost read: Elephant Runs Amok, 4 Die In Disaster!

In a tragic turn of events, a circus turned into a nightmare as Elsa, the nation's oldest performing elephant, went on a rampage. The chaos unfolded as the massive creature, once a beloved performer, broke free during the show, sending spectators into a frenzy of panic. Among the four dead, Mary Hennessey (12) was trampled by the mob escaping the collapsing tent and elephant. The incident has sparked a debate among animal rights activists and circus attendees: Should old elephants be allowed to perform in circus acts?

In a televised interview, Mary's father, Robert Hennessey, stood before the news crew, his lips quivering. "Elephants over a certain age should be retired from all circuses!" The wind ruffled his gray hair, and his eyes fought to hold back tears. "There must be laws to retire senior animals and prevent tragedies like this!" His gaze bored into the camera, releasing the floodgates.

Daniel Dewhurst retired from circus life in shame. He left without a proper sendoff, towing his egg camper north on US-277 toward Nebraska, knowing it would take roughly sixteen hours to get home. As the miles rolled by, he thought of Elsa, whose panic had turned the big top into a graveyard. He replayed the moment again and again; the snap of the tent pole, the screams, the stampede. The crew's faces haunted him. Their contemptuous stares made him question whether he truly belonged in their world. He drove in silence, the camper rattling behind him like a coffin on wheels.

During the journey, the first signs of throat complications reared their head. His voice grew hoarse, then raspy, then painful. Concerned, he scheduled a doctor's appointment as soon as he arrived home. In the weeks that followed, stabbing pains sent him through a maze of medical visits. Countless blood tests made him wonder if he had any left in his veins. Eventually, he was diagnosed with glottic carcinoma. Surgeons planned to remove his malignant tumor in his larynx and follow up with aggressive radiation treatments.

Though the surgery succeeded, radiation left his throat raw and ravaged. Insurance spared him financial ruin, but his body was only beginning to break. To further complicate matters, Daniel's health declined rapidly when he developed cirrhosis of the liver, a consequence of years of binge drinking. For the rest of his life, he would need to take synthetic sugar to control his ammonia levels. Day after day, Lactulose tethered him to the toilet, but at least his liver stayed happy.

The 4:05 train whistled to announce its arrival at the Hastings Burlington Station, echoing the town's origins as a late-1870s rail hub where locomotives once departed in five directions daily. Just south of the station, a call bell rang out, its sound drilling into Harriett Picoli's ears like an earwig burrowing into her brain. The way the clapper hit the bell, she swore it was the bong of Big Ben. She heaved her legs off the wicker coffee table, dislodging the stack of hardcover books that served as one leg.

The magazine she'd been avidly reading, featuring the best-dressed and worst-dressed celebrities, slammed onto the floor. She struggled to push up from the sagging, floral-print tuxedo sofa, cookie crumbs raining down. Assigned as caregiver to Daniel Dewhurst by Assuage Hospice Care (AHC), Gretchen stormed toward his room in her uneven, worn-down clogs. Her heavy steps imprinted on the carpet like bear prints in damp soil. She ricocheted down the hallway, her bouncy ringlets slapping her plump cheeks with each plodding step.

Lurching through the doorway, Gretchen barreled into the small, bland room, sending tremors through the walls. Daniel trembled. "Didn't I tell you not to ring the bell more than once? I heard you the first time!" she hollered, arching her left brow. "How do you expect me to clean the kitchen floor with you interrupting me every ten minutes?" Her eyes bored into his like hot pokers, branding him as her property. The flab under her arms jiggled when she planted her hands on her ample hips.

Daniel wished he could speak, but the larynx procedure left him with nothing but grunts and whimpers. *Better this than being dead.* Eyes pleading for mercy, he tried to make her realize he had rung the bell only once, but that was over twenty minutes ago! Daniel lay in bed with his legs crossed, holding his sizzling urine, as if keeping a shaken 2-liter soda bottle from exploding. Though he tried to resist, the urge was overpowering. He clenched his teeth, his face warping with strain. Suddenly, his eyes popped open.

And then it happened.

Gretchen's eyes grew wide. A questioning look. A look of disgust.

He let out a long sigh, and his eyes lost their focus. Everything about him softened, the grimace melting away like a ball of wax on a scorching day, replaced by a smile as relief flowed through him. The warm urine engulfed his senses like a macaque stumbling on a hot spring in the tundra, wiggling his wet rump deeper into the steam. But then the hot spring died, turning the warmth into bitter, chilling discomfort.

The moment hung in the air.

Gretchen knew precisely what had occurred. In an instant, the fearful look returned to his eyes—that I-did-something-wrong look. A look that knew a beating was in order. She understood the anatomy of the eyes. She was the eye whisperer. When people refused to speak, she relied on their portals to the soul to do the talking.

"Did you wet the bed again? Hmm?" Her voice carried that familiar dread.

Daniel flinched.

"I . . . told . . . you . . . not . . . to . . . wet . . . the . . . bed!" she yelled, her meaty hand slapping him upside the head with each word that spewed from her venomous mouth. Her face twisted with fury. Daniel whimpered and cringed against the barrage of blows, his eyes pleading for an end to the torment.

"Now I need to change the sheets again! Aren't you ashamed of yourself? You make me work *very* hard! I don't think that's fair, Daniel! Do *you* think that's fair?" she asked, her eyes bulging as if she were about to eat him whole. "Well . . . *do* you?"

Daniel looked confused. The deterioration of his memory had aligned with Gretchen's assignment as his aide. No matter how hard he tried to determine her motives for his harsh treatment, he failed to find any answers. Sometimes she overmedicated him, subjecting Daniel to relentless bouts of diarrhea. Other times, she skipped administering his medication because she was immersed in her tabloid magazines, crossword puzzles, and soap operas. On those days, which occurred with increasing frequency, the accumulated ammonia clouded his mind and dulled his motor skills. Even walking often seemed beyond his capacity. Collapsing to the floor only induced another round of beatings.

"Hello?! I can't wait a lifetime!" She grabbed his arm and pulled him up. With rough hands, she stripped off his soaked pajamas, plopped his feeble body on a metal folding chair, and left him trembling in his urine. The urine-drenched sheets were yanked off and flung into the hamper. A fresh sheet cracked as she snapped it in the air, parachuting over the bed. Gretchen never let up. She beat the bed into submission, aggressively tucking the ends of the sheet under the mattress.

* * *

Gretchen had always been bossy. She'd figured out it was easier to don a sizable magisterial crown and force others to do her bidding. But she was also crafty enough to fool people, including her supervisor, who found her delightful and competent in the interview. Her bright, cheerful attitude was a role she played only when necessary. Away from management's prying eyes, her true personality shone through. Gretchen's sneering and constant finger-pointing bred unease among her patients, more than any ulcer-causing bacterium gnawing at the stomach lining. Indeed, a more suitable name for her would have been Gretchen H. Pylori.

When a supervisor from AHC showed up unannounced for a routine check, his gaze lingered on the purple bruises mottling Daniel's skin. Lifting Daniel's arms, Jim traced the string of dark marks running down his shoulder and forearm.

"How on earth did this happen?" he asked.

"I was just as shocked as you are." Gretchen's lie flowed swiftly and naturally. "When I arrived yesterday morning, Mr. Dewhurst was struggling to get out of the bathtub. He tried to bathe without my assistance, even though I've repeatedly told him not to. But you know how much he loves to bathe."

Jim was clueless, but he nodded anyway.

"After I let myself in, I found Daniel slipping and sliding in the bathtub, so I rushed forward and grabbed his arm. I suppose my grip was a little too firm, but I only meant to keep him from drowning. A woman of my stature doesn't know her own strength. In fact, people often ask me if I've ever been a female wrestler." Gretchen grinned at her ingenuity. Her tale clicked into place, so neatly she almost believed it herself. She blinked, puckering her lips.

"Well, the answer is no, but I'm sure I could take down any woman twice my size." She thrust her hip toward him, and the supervisor grinned nervously. She approached Daniel, who lay stunned and helpless in his rumpled bed, and ran her fingers through his thinning hair.

"You should've seen him. He was slippery as a wet noodle! When I lost my grip, he fell and banged his arm against the bathtub. But don't worry. I'm well-trained in treating cuts and bruises. Once I got him out of the tub, I lectured him about the dangers of bathing without my assistance. That's my job. Isn't that right, Mr. Dewhurst?" Gretchen leaned in close and lifted her left eyebrow in warning.

Daniel's eyes focused on her sneering lips, and he recoiled from the hot breath that seared his face. He tried to make sense of the nonsense she'd spun, but it sounded like the mockingbird had stolen another song from a bird in flight. Nevertheless, he decided nodding was the prudent response.

"Great job, Gretchen," said Jim. "Our company needs more caregivers like you. I just need your signature to acknowledge my visit." He handed her his clipboard and a black felt-tip pen.

After signing the form with a smooth flourish, Gretchen showed the supervisor out and stormed back to the bedroom.

Daniel was a prisoner in his own home, unable

to escape or call for help. He shuddered as her stomps echoed throughout the house. *This is hell. I've done everything this woman has asked, but nothing satisfies her.*

Gretchen towered over the bed and struck the side of his head, each blow snapping his neck to the side. He whimpered, his head bobbing, trying to avoid the blows.

"Next time I ask you a question, I expect you to answer right away!" she bellowed, her voice reverberating in his ears.

Daniel turned his head away, his gaze settling on the blank wall. At least he didn't have to look at her bulging eyes that popped from their sockets every time she exploded. When she'd first arrived, he had thought Gretchen was like living inside an active volcano, unpredictable and perilous. Now, he thought it was more like standing before a raging bull.

Gretchen stormed out of the bedroom, neglecting Daniel's medication for the third consecutive time. This oversight allowed more toxins to seep into his bloodstream, further deteriorating his fragile mental state. Sometimes, he lay in bed confused and dazed, wondering where he was and how he got there. Other times, she overmedicated him, forcing Daniel to struggle toward the bathroom, gripping his walker for support while his body trembled under the strain.

Just after dawn, once the battered milk truck had rattled through tis route, Daniel's intestines churned wildly from the previous night's double dose of lactulose, rumbling like a snow-capped mountain on the verge of an avalanche. He tried to hold his bowel movement until Gretchen arrived, but the minutes dragged on.

Please hurry. I can't hold on much longer!

His eyes widened with fear and loathing as sweat poured from his forehead, soaking the pillow beneath him. *Tick. Tick. Tick.* The cheap plastic clock hung askew on the wall, its seconds dragging by. It read 7:46; only a minute had passed since he last looked. The pressure in his colon intensified; his eyes crossed as he clenched his sphincter muscles.

Though doubtful of success, Daniel realized the situation was untenable. He stared at the walker, willing it closer. *If only I could call it to me, like that masked man who whistles for his trusty horse.* He forced himself to sit, legs sliding over the bed's edge. His hand trembled as he reached for the walker. The farther he stretched, the more his fingers shook.

A deep, guttural growl.

He froze, waiting for his stomach's protests to subside before trying again. His heart raced, and his body shivered like a spider's web quivering under the weight of morning dew. Sweat trickled down his neck, soaking his flannel shirt as waves of anxiety and nausea gnawed at him. The looming threat of Gretchen's reprimand lingered at the edge of his thoughts. His fingers found purchase on the walker, and he pulled it close.

I did it!

He let out a long sigh.

Sliding off the bed, he landed off balance and teetered as the walker tipped dangerously. He had no time to spare. His heart pounded wildly as he lurched across the floor, unsteady as a toddler taking his first steps. The aluminum walker rattled in his haste, each step less stable than the last.

Left foot. Right foot.

Left foot. Right foot.

In response to his prayers, Daniel reached the bathroom with no time left. But the cool linoleum floor couldn't hold back the weight of snow rushing down the mountain slope. The surge became an avalanche, cascading down his hairy legs like muddy waters after a torrential downpour. He struggled to yank his soiled pajamas down, his feet zigzagging through the watery excrement until he hit the floor with a painful thump. Slipping from his grasp, the walker clattered against the toilet, then lay on its side, mocking him.

Gretchen H. Picoli entered the kitchen wearing the grin of someone freshly promoted. Caring for Dewhurst was effortless, and she had ensured her position as his caregiver by influencing assignment decisions. Setting her purse on the dining table, she strutted to Daniel's bedroom, lifting each leg as though marching through six inches of snow. When she reached the bedroom, a wave of confusion washed over her at the sight of the unmade bed and missing walker. She scowled. *What the hell is he up to now?* Her ears perked at faint sounds filtering in from the bathroom. Tilting her head, she listened intently. *Aha! There it is again!* It was the scraping of hollow metal against the floor.

Her generous body swayed as she burst through the bathroom door. In an instant, her face contorted into a grotesque spectacle: her eyeballs bulged, and the pupillary sphincter dilated so wide that a blinding halo momentarily overtook her vision. Veins in her temples popped like fireworks. Her jaw dropped, the disc snapping out of place. She couldn't decide whether to scream or collapse. Either way, cardiac arrest seemed preferable to cleaning up this mess!

"You son of a bitch!" she screeched, her

stinging tongue flapping like a tattered sail.

Daniel groveled in his excrement, trying to explain. What came out instead were dry, mule-like shrieks, raw with pain. A nurse's clog slammed into his ribcage with a sickening squelch, flipping him onto his side. Her foot jammed into his soiled buttocks before he crashed back down. Gretchen paused, pushed aside a ringlet of hair that blurred her vision, then smacked her lips and pulled up her sleeves. She resumed the assault. She kicked, and kicked, and kicked. The mule shrieked in pain with each blow.

The ex-clown thought she would never stop.

* * *

Friday, September 3, 2004. 8:25 p.m. Day of elephant incident. Evening show canceled.

The tent's interior was as dim as the dark side of the moon. When the man stepped inside, the temperature rose a few degrees, and the pale light over the washbasin illuminated the path to the oval mirror. His heavy footsteps kicked up dust, particles dancing in the light beams as he slowly approached. The mirror's frame curled with timeworn vines and dulled gold, whispering secrets only the past remembered.

He watched intently as his image faded, revealing a dark, luminous cloud that seemed to absorb all light around it. Shadows deepened, creeping closer, a darkness hungry for his soul. The demon's eyes were immense Tahitian pearls, shifting in place under crushing gravity, emitting an eerie, otherworldly glow. Only a twisted mockery of joy lived in those depths, as cold and sharp as a blade. It dwelled in a different dimension, trapped, waiting for the right moment to escape. Though its lips moved as it spoke, its words lagged several seconds, like a poorly dubbed line in a foreign film. The air thickened, suffused with impending doom, as though reality itself were fraying at the edges.

"Releasing the lion and unhitching the trailer went according to plan," the demon snickered, fogging up the mirror. "And hiding a pushpin in the saddle pad was a clever idea."

"Please forgive me for not keeping you better apprised, but there was very little time."

"You did well enough for a mortal. You serve the greater purpose." The creature's brows jumped in wonder, and its mouth gaped in a satisfied grin.

"You are the Doyen of Torture. The Grandmaster of Pain, oh Master," the man said, bowing. "Unfortunately, a young girl by the name of Mary Hennessey was trampled to death . . ."

"That's the easy way out!" the entity boomed, its face swelling tenfold, forcing newly formed jagged teeth against the glass.

The man jumped back as a sudden blast of anger erupted, kicking up dirt and swaying the tent walls like a fast-approaching storm.

"Death is quick and easy! I want slow, cruel torture that makes people cry out in mortal agony!"

The man shielded his face with his forearm before the sound wave could traverse the glass, eyes shut tight. His teeth clenched, lips tensed.

The floor trembled beneath him as the mirror jolted and swung on the single nail. The gust blew back his hair, sending him staggering.

When it subsided, the man cast his gaze into the mirror. The reflection revealed the despotic beast to be as ancient as the forbidden fruit, ageless as time itself. "Yes, Master. It shan't happen again," he replied, bowing his head.

"A pot boils only that which it contains; outside of that, the flames are an easy way out." As the Grandmaster of Pain retreated, its face shrank to fit within the frame's confines. "There have been many great moments in history when tormenting people was a thrill, an exciting game employing many forms of torture, but none gave me more pleasure than the era you mortals call medieval times." A peal of wicked laughter. A hearty sigh. "I hunger for those times. You must *recruit* more people. I have more torment to dispense," it cackled, fluttering the man's hair with each evil huff of laughter.

"Yes, Emperor of Agony."

As the man turned to leave, the demon's vicious tittering faded into the dimension from which it came. He stopped by the entrance, lifting his hat. Shoving the flap open, he stepped into the night, where the warm air wrapped its fingers.

A boy pedaling through the circus grounds skidded to a stop. "Hey, Mister, did you feel that tremor?"

Joe Milagro's eyes, as black as pestilence, searched the boy's angelic face. His top hat stood tall, and he jutted his chin, dusting off his long red coat. Its tail slithered like that of a plague-infested rat. "'Fraid not, young man. Say . . . Ever think about joining the circus?"

The boy's hazel eyes flashed with a glimmer of excitement.

ACKNOWLEDGMENTS

The Clown And The Caregiver was written between 2006 and 2008, long before the emergence of AI-assisted writing tools. In 2024, the author embraced these innovations to enhance the manuscript through selective drafting and editorial refinement. This manuscript reflects a collaborative process between the author and AI-assisted, with all final decisions and narrative direction remaining solely the author's.

I want to thank my beta reader and copy editor, Carissa Schlafer, of Carissa's Editorial Services, and my line editor, Ginny Ruths, Touchstone Publications, whose constructive feedback strengthened the story. In addition, any shortcomings that remain in the book after the editorial process are my own.

Chapter art generated by AI
Cover: Clown and Elephant Generated by AI
Cover design by Tea Jagodić.

ABOUT THE AUTHOR

Edgar spent the formative years of his life in Southern California, attending private schools. As a teen, he enjoyed reading horror and science fiction novels that explored utopian and dystopian ideas. He often wondered how a utopian society would come about. As a young adult, he noticed that most utopian and dystopian novels introduce readers to an unknown future without explaining its origin. Inspired by this, he wrote a story about a pre-utopian society on the cusp of becoming a great nation. Combining his love for fantasy, action, and suspense, he brings you an action-packed story that paves the path to a utopia. "Pay close attention," he says. "House of Broken Bones is a puzzle."

Edgar now lives in Ontario, California. He is retired and enjoys traveling and meeting with social clubs for karaoke, dining, and other fun activities.

X: @EdgarJHern12748

OTHER TITLES
AS CLEAR AS NIGHT
(A SHORT STORY)

As Clear As Night is a gripping tale about Alex Blackwell, a man who gains extraordinary abilities after a freak accident. He discovers that he can vanish and reappear unharmed in a different location, a revelation that leads him into a world of crime and deception, testing the limits of his power and morality. After a series of unsuccessful criminal activities, he turns to his girlfriend, Stacey, for help. However, she firmly refuses, insisting that his abilities should be used for the benefit of humankind rather than for corruption. When Stacey uncovers a dark secret about her own family, their lives become intertwined in a dangerous game of revenge and betrayal.

As their paths collide, they must confront the consequences of their actions and decide whether to use their powers for good or succumb to the darkness.

Collect all three covers.

OTHER TITLES
LIFEGIVER

(A SHORT STORY)

A turbulent birth in the Perseus spiral arm of the Milky Way sends a fragment of a dying star hurtling toward Earth. As the atmosphere strips away its outer layer, a lone flake drifts down into the heart of Miami's beachfront. In a twist of cosmic fate, young Herman Sinclair swallows the fragment and is forever changed.

Gifted—and cursed—with the power to bring inanimate objects to life with a touch, Herman's mother, Evelyn, works tirelessly to shield him from the public. For years, her vigilance keeps his abilities hidden. But when a moment of freedom in a bustling Miami mall sets chaos in motion, Herman's secret explodes into the open. This gripping tale of power, responsibility, and sacrifice probes

the human cost of extraordinary gifts and the chaos
unleashed by a single starry fragment.
Collect all three covers.

OTHER TITLES
HOUSE OF BROKEN BONES
(COMPLETE NOVEL)

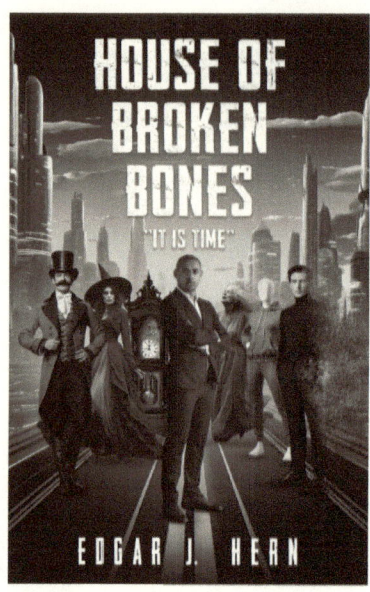

A collection of seven macabre and imaginative short stories that delve into the depths of human nature and the supernatural. From a man with the power to transport his physical body to a vengeful young woman who transforms into a wicked witch, these tales explore the extraordinary. A sinister circus plagued by sabotage, a grandfather clock with the ability to manipulate time, and a boy who breathes life into mannequins highlight the eerie and enigmatic. Additionally, a psychic girl fights to save the universe from implosion, and a provocative story examines the Senate's debate on eradicating money from society to combat the roots of evil. Each story is a piece of the puzzle, intricately interconnected to form a haunting tapestry.

www.ingramcontent.com/pod-product-compliance
Lightning Source LLC
Chambersburg PA
CBHW030606130626
46552CB00006B/2673